*American Frontier #9*

# ANNIE OAKLEY
# IN THE WILD WEST
# EXTRAVAGANZA!

**A Historical Novel**

by Ron Fontes and Justine Korman

Illustrations by Charlie Shaw

Cover illustration by Dave Henderson

DISNEY
PRESS
NEW YORK

Noelle

FIRST EDITION
1   3   5   7   9   10   8   6   4   2

Library of Congress Catalog Card Number: 93-70937
ISBN: 1-56282-491-0/1-56282-492-9 (lib. bdg.)

Consultant: Barbara Sklar Maslekoff, Librarian
Ohioana Library, Columbus, Ohio
Editor, *Ohioana Quarterly*

# CHAPTER 1

Annie Oakley caught her breath. Striding across the open air was a tall, handsome man in elaborately embroidered fringed buckskins and thigh-high leather boots. A diamond winked in the bright silk neckerchief knotted at his throat.

"Well, I do declare," Annie said. With his long brown hair and wide-brimmed Stetson and that droopy mustache and beard, he looked exactly like the pictures Annie had seen in all those newspapers and magazines. But this was no blurry drawing on faded newsprint, neither. No, siree. Immediately her heart set to pounding. It was him. William Frederick Cody. *Buffalo Bill* Cody.

Buffalo Bill stopped right in front of Annie, bowed gallantly, and smiled.

"Well, missie!" he said. "Let's see what you can do."

Annie's husband, Frank Butler, pressed a long rifle into Annie's hand.

"You're not much bigger than a speck.  Are you sure you can shoot that thing?" Buffalo Bill asked.

Frank winked at Annie.

"I can shoot, Mr. Cody," Annie assured him.

The Butlers' white poodle, George, gave a happy bark.  George loved being in show business and was eager to perform his part in the act.

Frank tossed six clay targets up into the air, one after the other, in a circle high above their heads.  In one smooth motion Annie lifted the rifle and fired—*BLAM! BLAM! BLAM!*—until each target exploded in a puff of dust.

George sat up on his haunches and held his front paws together as if he were clapping.  Buffalo Bill smiled.

Annie and Frank demonstrated the highlights of the sharpshooting routine they had worked out in vaudeville shows back east with the Sells Brothers Circus.  Even though she hadn't liked sharing the spotlight with two other rings, Annie had loved the circus.  The Butlers might have stayed in it for years, but bad weather had ruined the 1884 circus season, and the Sells brothers had no money to pay their performers.  Frank and Annie had decided to move on.

They were eager to audition for Buffalo Bill's Wild West.  Eastern audiences couldn't get enough of these real live demonstrations of life on the frontier.  And no doubt about it—of all the western extravaganzas, Buffalo Bill's Wild West was the biggest and best.

For Annie's next trick, Frank balanced an apple on

George's head. The fearless poodle waited patiently while Annie rode her horse around the ring—standing on her saddle. Annie swung her rifle up to her shoulder, took careful aim, and *BLAM!* The apple shattered, and George greedily gobbled a chunk of crisp fruit.

Now for the finale: Turning her back to Frank, Annie held up a wide-bladed knife. She slung her rifle backward over her shoulder, fixing her eyes on Frank's reflection in the knife's shiny blade.

Frank stood twenty-five paces across the ring, holding up a deck of cards. Each card was emblazoned with the name Annie and a bright red heart.

Annie squinted until her focus narrowed to the red heart in the center of the deck. Then she fired.

Frank tossed Buffalo Bill a card. He peered at Annie through the hole drilled straight through the printed heart.

"Next performance is in an hour," Buffalo Bill said matter-of-factly. "Be ready."

Frank smiled and draped his arm around her shoulder. "You made it!" he beamed.

"*We* made it!" Annie said. "Imagine it, Frank— Buffalo Bill's Wild West Show!"

"Don't call it a 'show,'" came a friendly warning.

Annie looked up. Standing before her was one of the biggest men she had ever seen.

The big man grinned and stuck out his hand. "The name's Bear," he said.

Annie and Frank had to laugh.

"Welcome to the Wild West," Bear said.

They shook hands. "You see," Bear explained, "Colonel Cody don't like anyone calling the Wild West a show on account of how authentic he tries to make it."

Annie nodded.

Bear led them on an informal tour of the compound. Frank and Annie agreed that in all their years performing they had never seen anything as elaborate as the Wild West.

"Looks more like a city," Annie said breathlessly. Bear smiled as if to agree.

Frank gave a low whistle. "I swear I've had more elbowroom in the center of a stampede!"

They all laughed.

Over there was the barbershop. And there the shoe-maker's. Fires smoldered at another tent where Annie heard the *clang clang* of a blacksmith's hammer.

Cowboys strutted from tents to corrals, silver spurs jangling from the heels of their tall boots. Annie stopped to admire a team of beautifully groomed horses.

There were deer, bear, buffalo, and bucking broncos, too. George whimpered at the sight of a giant moose quietly chewing apples. Annie patted his head reassuringly. "Don't fret, George," she said. The fact is, she had never seen a moose, either, and its enormous antlers were rather alarming.

Bear gestured toward a group of men wearing elaborate feather headdresses. "They're Wichita and Pawnee tribesmen," he said.

Some of the men called to each other in their native languages. Others spoke English. Two young men played table tennis as a crowd of excited onlookers hastily placed their bets.

Bear nodded to a lone tribesman sitting as still as a statue before a white canvas tent. "That there is Sitting Bull," he said.

The great Sioux chief dipped his head ever so slightly in their direction. Annie was thrilled. *Sitting Bull*—this was the very man who had led his people against General Custer at Little Bighorn! Annie knew it was rude to stare, but she risked a glance over her shoulder at the proud head that topped those massive shoulders.

"Sitting Bull is big medicine," Bear said.

Annie wasn't sure what Bear meant by "big medicine," but she could feel the strength and dignity surrounding the old chief.

Bear opened the flap of a nearby tent and said, "This is where you'll be staying."

Annie peeked inside. Sunlight filtered through the white canvas, lending a warm glow to the flower-patterned wool rug that covered the wooden floor. Two folding cots lined the sides of the room. There were also several canvas chairs, a table, and a collapsible canvas bathtub.

Annie grinned at Frank. This was certainly a step up from their tent in the Sells Brothers Circus and a long way from the dingy hotel rooms they had shared in their vaudeville days.

"If you need anything, just give a holler," Bear said.

Annie shook his giant hand and smiled warmly. The flesh above Bear's thick beard blushed pink.

# CHAPTER 2

Annie looked up into the clear blue sky and smiled.
She and Frank had seen enough rain to last a life-
time—maybe two lifetimes. But today there wasn't
a cloud to be seen for miles!

Frank squeezed Annie's hand and, as if reading her
mind, said, "Nothing's going to rain on your parade
today, Little Girl."

Annie smiled at the familiar nickname. Growing
up, Annie had resented being smaller than most of the
other children, but now she no longer cared. At six feet,
Frank stood a full foot taller than Annie. When she
needed to she could lean against his broad shoulder and
feel safe. More important, Annie had proved more than
once that she was capable of taking care of herself.

"You'll go on right after the Grand Promenade, missie," Buffalo Bill told her as he led his white horse to the
entrance area just outside the ring. The great showman
looked magnificent in embroidered buckskins and shining
boots. His horse sparkled with a gold braid and a
studded harness.

Annie nodded, heart thumping with excitement.

"You and Frank can ride in this carriage in the promenade," Buffalo Bill said. He showed them a little carriage drawn by a matching pair of mustang horses. Annie patted their tawny necks and admired the tidy braiding of their black manes.

Buffalo Bill consulted a gold pocket watch, then grinned. "No sense keeping folks waiting!" He swung into the ornate saddle of his beautiful white stallion and rode out into the open-air ring.

Canvas canopies shaded the excited spectators filling the circle of bleachers around the ring.

Annie's ears were used to gunshots, but she was startled by the thunderous roar of applause that erupted when Buffalo Bill galloped out to greet the crowd. The cheers were followed by rousing music coming from the bandwagon carrying the brass band in its crimson and gold-braided uniforms. Six white horses pulled the wagon, lifting their hooves in time to the booming bass drum.

War whoops echoed as the Pawnee braves rode into the ring on bucking broncos. Annie gasped at the sight of their leader in a magnificent eagle-feather headdress.

The vaqueros—Mexican cowboys—rode out next in their dashing flat black hats and wide trousers. When the American cowboys rode out, whooping and hollering, the crowd cheered even louder.

Then it was Annie and Frank's turn to ride into the ring. The mustangs knew where to go and lifted their hooves in a stately walk. Annie could not take her eyes off the cheering throng of fifteen hundred people.

"Where did they all come from?" she wondered.

"This must be everyone in the town and for miles around," Frank said.

Annie agreed. Young and old, rich and poor, the townsfolk had put aside work, school, and chores for the chance to see Buffalo Bill's Wild West. Annie smiled and waved, and the cheers rumbled like thunder.

When the Grand Promenade was over, Annie waited nervously for Buffalo Bill to finish greeting the audience and announce her act.

"Land sakes, who ever heard of a woman sharp-shooter?" A tinny voice close at hand made Annie turn around. An old man was talking to Bear.

"It's unnatural, I tell ye," the old man said. He tugged in distress at his bushy, old-fashioned side-whiskers. "The next thing you know, they'll be chawin' tobacky and wantin' the vote!"

Bear looked over the old man's stooped shoulders. His eyes met Annie's, and he shrugged.

"I've got work to do, Mr. McCluskey," Bear said.

The old man's frown deepened. "Sure you do. The show must go on, even if it means starring a girl who can barely lift a rifle!"

He stalked off, still grumbling.

Annie's heart sank. The Grand Promenade had been so spectacular, and out there was the biggest crowd she had ever seen, not to mention Buffalo Bill himself. Maybe the old man was right. Maybe little Phoebe Anne Moses had no place in this grand arena.

Frank put his hand on Annie's shoulder and tilted up her chin so he could look into her eyes. "Come on! It's time to show that old man just how wrong he is!"

Annie's good cheer and confidence returned like sunshine when the clouds blow away. She swung into the saddle of a fine spotted pony and gave her rifle another quick check.

Frank smiled and mounted a dappled gray mare.

"And now," came the voice of Buffalo Bill, "I have a very special treat for you."

An excited murmur spread through the bleachers. Everyone eagerly craned their necks and leaned to one side and another to get the best view of the ring.

"In her first performance with the Wild West, I give you the foremost woman sharpshooter in the world, the Little Girl of the Western Plains—Miss Annie Oakley!"

*The Little Girl of the Western Plains!* As anxious as she was, Annie had to chuckle. I'm from Ohio, she thought. I've never even been west of the Mississippi River! So this, Annie thought, was show business—*Wild West* style. It felt wonderful.

The crowd cheered as Annie's pinto pony pranced into the ring. Sunlight winked off the many prize medals decorating her Western-style shirt. She waved her wide-brimmed Stetson.

"Yeehah! Yippee! Yaahooo!" the spectators roared. Annie thought her heart would thump right out of her chest.

"Ready, Little Girl?" Frank whispered. He gave her hand a squeeze.

Annie nodded. She spurred the pony again and rode around the big ring. She jumped off her horse and leapt over a table that held a rack of rifles. In an instant, one rifle was in her hands.

Frank tossed up six glass balls. *BAM!* The first exploded in a shower of tinkling glass. The crowd gasped.

Annie picked up another rifle. *BAM!* And another and another. *BAM! BAM!* More glass balls exploded into shiny fragments in the dust.

Next, Frank tossed a playing card high in the air. Before it floated to earth, Annie had drilled ten holes in it.

Then, while the crowd was still catching its breath, she shot the apple off George's head. The poodle ran around in delighted circles while the spectators whistled and clapped.

Frank swung a glass ball on a string until the clear sphere was a blur of shiny motion. The hypnotized crowd held its breath.

Annie squinted her eyes until all she saw was the shimmering ball. She squeezed the trigger. The rifle blast was followed instantly by the tinkling of shattered glass.

Before the cheers could die down, Frank held up a deck of their special cards. With one sure shot, Annie drilled through the heart of the first card and all the way through the deck.

As Frank tossed cards to the awestruck audience,

Annie curtsied and waved her big hat once more. The people clapped and whistled and stamped their boots on the wooden bleachers.

When she rode out of the ring, Annie heard a man joyously shout, *"Wantanyeya ciscila!"*

She turned and saw Sitting Bull. His dark eyes glowed. *"Wantanyeya ciscila,"* he repeated.

Annie swelled with pride. The words didn't make any sense to her, but Annie understood from the way they were spoken that they came from the heart.

Frank took George back to their tent. Then he and Annie sat in the bleachers for the rest of the show. In a replica of an authentic village, Pawnee, Sioux, and Wichita tribesmen demonstrated their horse-riding skills.

Then the tribesmen folded their tepees and moved their village, just as they used to when roving freely over the prairie. A pioneer wagon train rocked and rolled into the ring. Cows lumbered along behind the wagons. Pots and pans clanged on pegs along their wooden sides.

Annie was nearly shaken out of her seat by the pounding hoofbeats of a herd of buffalo. It was Buffalo Bill himself who was chasing the huge beasts around and around the arena. Finally, he herded them out of the ring. Frank coughed at the huge cloud of dust.

Next came the fearless riders of the pony express. Skilled horsemen reenacted the daring deeds of the young messengers who had opened a line of communication with the Far West.

Then, with six-guns blazing and lassos swinging, cowboys chased a herd of longhorn cattle into the arena. Led by huge Buck Taylor, the King of the Cowboys, they rounded up and roped each and every dogie. "Those crazy cowboys are louder than a pack of starving coyotes!" Frank shouted. Annie agreed. "Probably hear them coming clear through to Wyoming!" They both laughed like happy children.

For Annie the most exciting part was the reenactment of the battle for the Deadwood Stage. She remembered reading that Buffalo Bill had bought the actual stagecoach that used to run through the North Dakota mining boomtown with its shipment of gold that made a favorite target for bandits.

Each performance, several cowboys rode the rattling stagecoach across the ring until they were "attacked" by "wild Indians." Arrows zinged through the air thick and fast as pounding hooves and harrowing war cries shocked the crowd. The cowboys fired blanks at their attackers, who fell spectacularly from their ponies to roll in the dust.

For a moment Annie forgot she was sitting on bleachers, safe and sound. She imagined herself on the desolate plains, one stagecoach and a few guns away from death.

Annie's throat felt dry with the dust stirred up by all the hooves and wheels. A cloud of gunsmoke drifted up from the ring and into the clear blue sky.

Annie was awed by the courage of the cowboys and

was thrilled each time a bullet struck its mark. And when the few remaining attackers rode off carrying their "dead," Annie was flushed with joy and relief. She felt a little embarrassed until she looked around and saw the same expression on other faces in the crowd. Now she knew why Buffalo Bill refused to call his Wild West a "show." It was so much more than that!

# CHAPTER 3

**T**he compound felt quiet and empty after the last of the crowd had gone. A bell rang, and the exhausted performers drifted toward the big mess tent to eat. Annie suddenly realized she was famished.

"That was some mighty fine shooting you did out there!"

Annie knew without looking that the voice behind her belonged to Buffalo Bill.

"I'd say you've earned some supper."

All the way to the mess tent, Buffalo Bill introduced Annie and Frank to the crew and the other performers. Annie felt dizzy with all the new names.

Right away she knew there were two names she would never forget. One belonged to a small, wiry cowboy not much bigger than herself. Annie remembered that in the fight to defend the Deadwood Stage, he had been the most ferocious.

"Eugene Francis Marsh," the man said with an awkward bow. "But most folks just call me Shorty. You can, too, if you want, ma'am."

Annie smiled, and the cowboy blushed and stepped aside to let his tall companion speak.

"John Henry Colt," the man stammered. "But around here I'm known as Colorado Jack." The lanky, freckled cowboy swiped off his hat to reveal a tumble of red curls. "M-m-mighty honored to make your acquaintance, ma'am." Then he bowed, bumped into Shorty, and backed away, tripping over his own spurs.

As they reached the mess tent, Annie inhaled the delightful odor of simmering stew. A cook in a long white apron stirred the stew with a spoon so big it looked like a pot at the end of a broom handle. Huge stew kettles hung from a sturdy wooden frame above a long open fire.

The cook's face was red with steam and effort. His bald head gleamed with sweat. The man looked up as Buffalo Bill approached.

"I'd like you to meet our new sharpshooter, Miss Annie Oakley, and her husband, Frank Butler," Buffalo Bill said.

The cook hastily wiped his hands on his apron and mopped his bald head with a white handkerchief. He extended a large, warm hand to Annie.

Buffalo Bill said, "Annie, this is our chief cook, Curly."

Annie's brown eyes darted from Buffalo Bill to the bald-headed man. Laughter sprang to her lips before she could shut them. "I . . . I'm . . ." Annie tried to apologize, but she couldn't stop laughing. I must! she thought desperately. If I get on the wrong side of the camp cook, we'll starve!

But to her great relief, Curly's pink face beamed with a delighted grin. "In my younger days I had a mop of blond curls," he explained. Then he patted his smooth head. "Now all I have left is the nickname." They all burst into laughter.

Inside, hundreds of performers and crew members crowded the long tables. Waiters hoisted heaping platters of biscuits and huge tureens of stew. A din of happy chatter and clanging spoons echoed inside the canvas walls.

Annie and Frank slid onto a bench beside Buffalo Bill. A man already seated at the table quickly rose and bowed.

"John Burke, our publicity agent," Buffalo Bill announced.

Burke wore a stylish double-breasted frock coat. His luxurious, perfumed brown hair flowed over his shoulders. Burke took Annie's hand in his and gently kissed her fingers as he bowed again.

"The Wild West is graced by your charming presence," Burke said in a smooth baritone. Now it was Annie's turn to blush.

While they ate, Burke discussed the plans he and Buffalo Bill had for the Wild West. "Once we complete our tour of New England, we will turn north to Canada, and finally on to the Midwest. After that, we have even more illustrious plans!"

As he listened, Buffalo Bill inclined his head to the right. Cody had been deaf in his left ear ever since he froze his eardrum while rescuing General Penrose's cavalry in a blizzard.

Burke waved his fork grandly. "Our friends across the Atlantic grow more fascinated by the American frontier every day." Burke lowered his voice dramatically. "In his youth, you see, Colonel Cody guided some of the crowned heads of Europe on perilous buffalo hunts across the rolling prairie of this great nation."

Buffalo Bill flashed Annie a modest smile. "Merely a grand duke or two. Terrible shots. But I made them Russians feel like mountain men."

Burke grasped the lapels of his coat. His chest filled with air for another blast. "Since the nobility made this pilgrimage west, we shall take the Wild West to Europe—culminating in a spectacular performance in honor of Queen Victoria's Golden Jubilee in 1887."

Buffalo Bill chuckled warmly. "That gives John two years to convince the British they want to see cowboys and Indians."

"Oh, but they already do!" Burke said excitedly.

Annie's eyes glazed over. To go to Europe! To perform for the queen! Not bad for a girl from Ohio! she thought.

Then Annie turned and saw the old man who had been grumbling with Bear before the performance. With all the excitement, she had almost forgotten about him. He glared at her with such cold hatred, Annie was forced to look away.

"Who is that?" she asked.

Buffalo Bill sighed. John Burke lit a fat cigar and shrank behind a cloud of blue smoke.

"That is Hugh McCluskey, former champion rifle shot of the world," Buffalo Bill finally said.

Annie glanced quickly at the old man hunched over his stew and then back to Buffalo Bill. "I replaced him, didn't I?"

Cody nodded. "McCluskey's eyes have been going for a long time. He missed his mark once too often."

Annie shook her head sadly. She was only twenty-five, and already her hearing was growing fainter because of all the gunshots. Losing her hearing she could accept. Losing one's eyesight, however, was something every sharpshooter dreaded.

"Hugh has a job with the Wild West for as long as he wants one," Buffalo Bill declared. His blue eyes were warm with compassion.

John Burke frowned. "A pitiful plight indeed. He has no family and no interests outside of show business."

Buffalo Bill agreed. "I can't say I ever recall him taking a season off or spending his salary on anything but gunpowder and bullets."

The old man handed his empty plate to a passing waiter, then stood to brush the crumbs off his black coat. None of the people busily chatting around McCluskey took any notice of his exit. Annie felt a twinge of sympathy for the old man.

Suddenly McCluskey's clouded gray eyes bored into her. Annie tugged Frank's sleeve.

Buffalo Bill looked nervous as the old man approached. He arranged his spoon and mug on his empty plate, and his eyes drifted longingly toward the open tent flap. But a broad smile quickly lit his handsome features as he rose and boomed, "Hugh McCluskey! I'd like you to meet our new sharpshooter, Miss Annie Oakley, and her husband, Frank Butler."

McCluskey's gnarled hand squeezed Annie's. His skin was as wrinkled and dry as a lizard's.

"Saw yer act," he said. "Not bad . . . fer a woman."

Annie's back stiffened. *Why did he have to make such an issue of her being a woman?* Rifles didn't care who pulled the trigger. Maybe that's why she liked them so much!

Frank broke the awkward silence by replying, "Nice of you to say so."

Annie smiled. "Yes, thank you, Mr. McCluskey. That's quite a compliment, coming from you."

McCluskey's grin revealed a row of tobacco-stained teeth. "Never heard of a sharpshooting act with a dog in it."

His gray eyes flickered over Cody and Burke, then he whispered confidentially to Annie and Frank, "Why don't you come by my tent sometime? I could give you a few pointers on improving your act. Then you wouldn't need that critter."

Now it was Frank's turn to get angry. George wasn't there to cover a lack of talent. He helped make their act special, which was plenty special judging by the cheers of the crowd. And he wasn't a *critter*, and how dare this old man . . .

John Burke stepped between Frank and McCluskey before any harsh words could be exchanged. "I would not presume to speak for them, except that I am certain Mr. and Mrs. Butler will want to settle in before they do any visiting," Burke said smoothly.

There was a hint of worry in Buffalo Bill's blue eyes as he studied McCluskey's face. The old man just nodded. "Plenty of time. I'm not goin' anywhere, except the grave."

Buffalo Bill slapped McCluskey on the back. "Well, I hope you aren't in any rush to do that. We still need you around here."

Annie sighed and realized she'd been holding her breath ever since the old man had extended his "invitation."

Buffalo Bill herded them all to the tent's opening. Annie felt relieved when the old man nodded and walked away. Burke bowed, and Buffalo Bill tipped his hat.

"One more thing," Annie said suddenly. "I was wondering, what does *Wantan* . . . oh, I forget. It was something Sitting Bull shouted after my act."

"Why don't you ask him yourself?" Buffalo Bill suggested. Annie turned and found herself face-to-face with the great Sioux chief.

"*Wantanyeya ciscila* means 'Little Sure Shot' in the language of my people," Sitting Bull explained.

Burke's eyes widened, and he snatched a small pad and pencil from his waistcoat pocket. "Little Sure Shot," he muttered, scribbling. "I like that."

Annie grinned. "So do I."

CHAPTER 4

Annie quickly adjusted to the Wild West's schedule. John Burke and Buffalo Bill had carefully choreographed each and every routine down to the smallest detail. There was a joke common among the performers that no one even blinked without Colonel Cody's approval.

When it was time to move on, the city of tents and bleachers disappeared inside the brightly painted Wild West train like a magician's assistant vanishing inside a folding box.

The train's ear-piercing whistle would toot twice, then it panted, *CHUF CHUF CHUF*, a big black iron ox pulling a heavy wagon. Then the locomotive would pick up speed, and soon they were gliding down the shimmering rails!

Annie never tired of the excitement of seeing new places. She especially loved the chugging Wild West train, with its great belches of black smoke and its lonely whistle.

Frank dozed peacefully on the worn leather seat opposite Annie. The card game in the corner of the car grew noisy with Shorty's victory whoop and Colorado Jack's disgruntled murmur. The other players made prairie-style jokes and exchanged tall tales and friendly insults. Sitting Bull placidly sucked a peppermint candy, watching the scenery whip past as if the loud cowboys did not exist.

An advance team traveled ahead of the Wild West like scouts before a conquering army. They made sure the field, racetrack, or park was ready for the Wild West's tents and grandstand and that necessary shipments of food and other supplies would be waiting.

The advance team plastered each town with posters announcing:

The West at Your Doors! More Scouts! More Skillful Marksmen and Markswomen! More Genuine Indians! More Western Animals! More Cowboys! More Wild Bucking Horses! The Largest Herd of Buffalo on the Continent!

One poster featured a huge buffalo with Cody's picture on its hump. Huge letters proclaimed: I Am Coming!

By the time the Wild West's train chugged toward town, folks were in a frenzy to see it.

When the train arrived at the next tour stop, the magic act reversed itself. Within a few very busy hours the empty field became the bustling tent city as Bear and his crew unpacked more than two dozen railroad cars that held the Wild West performers, animals, sets, props, and machinery.

Frank and one of the roustabouts carried Annie's special travel trunk. Its four drawers were exactly the right length for her short, homemade costumes. And the top folded up to make a dresser mirror.

Annie's sewing machine fit in a separate trunk, along with Frank's portable writing desk and George's favorite velvet cushion. Though they traveled constantly, wherever the Butlers went became a cozy home.

After the compound was set up, Buffalo Bill Cody led a grand parade through the town or city. The bandwagon thumped out cheerful music. Businesses shut their doors, and the streets filled with excited people swaying and marching to the beat. Children and dogs chased the wagons and prancing horses.

The advance team encouraged people to come early so they could see the performers in their tents, get a close look at the animals, soak up the Western atmosphere— and, of course, buy souvenirs.

Annie loved to watch wide-eyed children stare at their first sight of a real live cowboy or a big buffalo. The children loved to play with George. The poodle ate up every scrap of attention as Annie took him for his afternoon walk.

But not all the spectators were so friendly. Some people jeered at Sitting Bull as he sat outside his tent selling autographed photos.

Annie stopped when she heard a man shout rudely, "This no good Injun killed General Custer!"

Sitting Bull spoke with quiet calm. "I have answered to my people for the Sioux slain in that fight. The chief that sent Custer must answer to his people."

The man spat at Sitting Bull. Annie's fists clenched with rage. She stepped between the man and the chief. George growled. The man sneered, then walked away.

"Wantanyeya ciscila," Sitting Bull said. "You have the grace and courage of my beloved daughter, who is lost to me."

Annie saw tears sparkle in the old chief's eyes. She knew what it meant to lose someone you loved.

Sitting Bull patted George's head, then smiled at Annie. Even though Annie and Sitting Bull came from different worlds, she could not believe how close she felt to the old Sioux chief. "Thank you," she said simply.

Later, when Annie bumped into Bear outside the shoemaker's tent, she asked him why Sitting Bull was in the Wild West.

"He's gotta earn a living like anyone else," Bear explained. "I heard he has a couple of wives back on the reservation and eleven children, plus a bunch he adopted. Can't feed all of them on what the government gives."

Annie shook her head sympathetically.

"He has a good deal with Colonel Cody," Bear went on. "Got it written in his contract that he keeps all the money he makes selling his pictures." Bear shrugged. "Colonel Cody always honors a contract. It doesn't matter who you are or what color your skin. There's something about Buffalo Bill that just makes you glad to be alive. The man has a heart as wide open as the prairie."

Bear grinned. "Well, that's my speech for today. I best be gettin' along now."

Annie drifted back to her tent expecting to have a little time to relax and brush George before the second performance. She and Frank always liked the poodle to look good.

But no eager bark greeted her entrance. No wet nose pushed itself into her hand. George's velvet cushion sat on top of the sewing trunk, but the dog was nowhere in sight.

It wasn't like George to just wander off. Annie paced about the room with the dog brush in her hand. Maybe Frank's table tennis game ended early and he decided to take George for an extra walk, she thought.

Just then Frank appeared in the open tent flap, counting a wad of small bills.

"I won!" he said with a big grin. Annie's face looked troubled. "Don't tell me you disapprove of a little table tennis betting."

Then he looked around the tent. "Where's George?"

"That's what I've been wondering," Annie said. "He was napping on his cushion when I went to the shoemaker's tent to drop off your boots. I talked to Bear for a while, and when I came back, he was gone!"

Frank consulted his pocket watch. "We've got only fifteen minutes till the parade. I'll go east, you go west. Then we'll meet back here."

Without another word Frank strode out of the tent calling, "George!" at the top of his lungs.

Annie shouted, too. She asked everyone she passed if they had seen the poodle, but no one had.

"You're heading the wrong way, missie!" Buffalo Bill said.

Annie knew she should be at the arena with the other performers, but she had to meet Frank first.

Frank's face fell when he saw Annie alone. "We'll have to do the show without him," Frank decided. "And then we'll turn every tent upside down until we find him!"

Annie squeezed his hand. She loved George as much as Frank did, even though he had been Frank's dog before they met. Where could George be?

"You cut that awfully close," Buffalo Bill said a bit harshly as Annie and Frank arrived breathlessly at the arena. "I don't like to hold the opening parade for anyone."

Frank apologized while Annie checked her rifles. Out of the corner of her eye she saw Hugh McCluskey smirking. Then she saw a white head bobbing through a sea of knees.

"George!" Annie cried joyfully. The poodle leapt into her arms, tail wagging, tongue lapping. A ragged rope hung from his neck.

Frank examined the damp, frayed rope end and said, "He must've chewed himself free."

Frank ruffled the poodle's fur. "That's our George! He didn't want to miss a performance! But someone sure wanted him to."

Annie gave Frank a worried look. "Maybe so. But who?"

# CHAPTER 5

**F**rank had an idea who might want to sabotage the act: McCluskey. Annie thought about it, and it began to make sense. "But we have no proof," she told Frank, "and the old man would just deny it."

"You're probably right," Frank said. Then he patted George's head. "Maybe the best thing to do is to just ignore him."

Unfortunately, ignoring Hugh McCluskey was not as easy as the Butlers had hoped. The old man had few responsibilities—but plenty of time to make trouble.

"She isn't really making all those shots," Annie heard him grumble to Bear one evening outside the mess tent. "Those cards are drilled before the show. She's just shooting blanks."

Annie's ears burned with rage. Of course Bear didn't believe him, but how dare McCluskey tell such lies!

Soon after that, Annie was hanging her laundry up to dry when McCluskey walked by with a group of cowboys.

"I think it's mighty suspicious," McCluskey muttered, "that she calls herself Annie Oakley when her proper married name is Butler."

"Frank told me it's because some circuses won't hire family acts like Butler & Butler," Shorty piped up.

"Still seems fishy to me," McCluskey said as the men walked out of earshot.

Annie's arms dropped to her sides.

"Wantanyeya ciscila," a friendly voice called. "You look like you could use some stew."

Annie smiled. Now that Sitting Bull mentioned it, the supper she'd eaten just an hour before seemed to have evaporated in her stomach. That's what she got for spending her days riding, running, and jumping.

A pot of stew simmered over a small fire in front of Sitting Bull's tent.

"Sit," the chief said.

Annie sat on the woven blanket spread before the open tent.

"What troubles you?" the old chief asked.

Annie laughed. Sitting Bull could see right through to her feelings, just like Frank could. "Why do people make such a fuss about names?" Annie blurted.

Sitting Bull stirred the bubbling stew. The aroma made her mouth water.

"Names mean a great deal," Sitting Bull said at last. "Your name is who you are."

Annie didn't know what the old chief meant. A name was just a word, wasn't it? Sitting Bull saw meaning in everything, from dreams to the flight of birds.

They were all part of *Wakan' Tanka*—the Great Mysterious.

Sitting Bull stirred the stew, and for a time the two sat in companionable silence.

"My first name isn't really Annie," she confessed. Suddenly she wondered if McCluskey was right after all. Maybe she was just a fake. Her first name wasn't really her first name, and neither was her last. Annie shook the foolishness out of her head. Her bullets were real, and her aim was true. "I was born Phoebe Anne Moses," Annie explained. "But I hated the name Phoebe, so everyone called me Annie."

Sitting Bull smiled and ladled stew into a bowl. "You have always had a strong will, my daughter."

Annie giggled. That was true. Annie's mother had forbidden her to fire her father's rifle. But Annie had been determined to do more than just clean the weapon. She wanted to shoot—so she did!

"After my father and first stepfather died, I went to work for my mother's friend who was running a poor-house," Annie explained. "I was supposed to get food and clothing and a chance to go to school, since there wasn't any school near our cabin. But I was too busy helping to care for the old and sick inmates to have much time to learn anything except how to sew."

Sitting Bull sat so still that Annie waited for his eyes to blink before she continued, to make sure he hadn't fallen asleep with his eyes open.

"I didn't mind the work, but the poorhouse children

teased me all the time," Annie recalled with a shudder. "I think they were jealous because I was only *working* there. I still had a family and a real home—even if it was just a one-room log cabin."

Sitting Bull nodded.

"They used to dance around me and chant, 'Moses Poses,' over and over."

"What does that mean?" Sitting Bull asked.

Annie laughed. The taunt that had once made her so angry really didn't mean anything at all. She shrugged. "They were just making fun of my last name."

"Children will do that," Sitting Bull agreed.

"Well, it bothered me so much that when another job came up, I took it," Annie said. "A farmer and his wife promised to pay me fifty cents a week to help them take care of their baby. They also promised that I could go to school. But they worked me like a slave from sunrise to dark doing all the chores on their farm. I never went to school, and they never paid me a cent."

Sitting Bull shook his head. "To love money so much you would cheat a child. This is an evil thing."

"One morning, I ran away." Annie remembered the train that had carried her from that awful farm back home. What joy she had felt when the first familiar sights had sped past the smoke-blurred window. No wonder she still loved trains!

"When I got home, my mother had married again, and my older sisters were married and gone," Annie said.

How strange it had been not to see Lyda, Mary Jane, Elizabeth, and Mary Ellen. But how wonderful to be home!

Annie continued. "My mother's new husband was a kind man, but he had no head for business. There was a big mortgage on the farm, and if we didn't pay up, we would lose our home."

Sitting Bull's hands curled into fists, then relaxed again. "They would take the land from under your feet," he said sadly.

"That was when I learned to shoot," Annie recalled with a smile. "And when I earned enough money to pay the mortgage, I changed my last name to Mozee." She laughed. It seemed silly now to have changed her dear father's name just because of some teasing children, but at the time it had seemed a move toward independence and freedom from poverty.

Besides, Annie had always liked the way the French gentleman who owned the ammunition store back home pronounced her name. Mozee—it sounded romantic.

"When I married Frank, I became Mrs. Butler." Annie's eyes glowed with love. "But Butler & Butler wasn't a good name for our vaudeville act, so I picked Oakley."

Annie's cheeks flushed with the sweet memory of ten years before. She had been only fifteen, on her first trip to Cincinnati, visiting Lyda and her husband, Joe. Annie had never seen such an enormous town.

And then Lyda and Joe took her to the suburb of Oakley above the city. Annie was dazzled by the view.

The buildings looked like toys from that height, and there were so many of them!

Then there had been the contest against the big smiling man in the shooting jacket and soft green hat. One look in Frank's kind blue eyes and Annie knew, here was someone special!

"Frank and I met in a suburb of Cincinnati called Oakley. I loved the name," Annie finally said.

Sitting Bull smiled.

"And now, thanks to you, I have a new name," Annie said brightly. "My Wild West name—Little Sure Shot."

Annie said good-bye to Sitting Bull and, full of warm stew and good feelings, walked back to her tent. Hugh McCluskey's nasty words seemed as far away as the taunts of the children in the poorhouse.

Annie had a wonderful name and a wonderful life! She fell asleep feeling like the luckiest young woman in the world and wondering if there was some way she could repay the Great Mysterious for her good fortune.

CHAPTER
6

fter the first performance the next day, Annie got
her answer. The excited squeals of many children
drew her attention to Sitting Bull's tent. The great
chief stood outside, surrounded by ragged newsboys and
bootblacks. He looked like a rich, happy grandfather as
he tossed coins and candy to the delighted boys.

Annie's practical side frowned. Here was Sitting
Bull, with eleven of his own children, not to mention the
ones he had adopted, all waiting at home for him on the
reservation while he scattered his salary to these dirt-
smudged orphans he would probably never see again.
And yet Annie could not help but be moved by the joy
on the chief's face.

"How can the white man leave his children to
starve?" Sitting Bull asked when the boys had finally
gone.

Annie shook her head. After spending so much time
with Sitting Bull she was beginning to think white people
were pretty strange herself!

"There are orphanages," Annie said.

Sitting Bull replied, "These boys tell me they would rather live on their own."

Annie couldn't blame them, recalling the dismal poorhouse where she had sewed and cleaned. Sitting Bull, who had refused to live on the reservation, of course understood why the boys would rather spend their nights shivering with growling stomachs than live in a "home" that was more like a prison.

"I wish I could take them all home," Sitting Bull said. "But home is not as it was in the old days. There are not enough buffalo for our tribe, and the children cannot grow strong on scraps of government meat."

Annie nodded. "I wish there was something I could do, too." Then she sighed and thought, But all I know how to do is perform in a show. An idea came to her. That was it! If she couldn't provide homes for all these orphaned children, she could at least bring a little joy into their lives.

"Where are you going, my daughter?" Sitting Bull called after Annie, who was walking with such speed and determination that she did not hear him. Annie did not stop until she found Buffalo Bill and John Burke smoking cigars in the treasury tent.

Burke was leaning his chair back against the square black metal safe. A pinky ring glittered on the chubby hand that held his smoldering cigar. At the sight of Annie, Burke politely got to his feet.

Buffalo Bill rose from his chair, his long, drooping

mustache lifting with his smile. "What can we do for you, missie?" Cody cocked his head so his good ear would be closer to Annie.

Annie was so excited her face nearly glowed. "I think we should give away free tickets to orphanages."

The two men puffed their cigars in silence. Burke squinted suspiciously at Annie and then carefully examined Bill Cody's reaction. The colonel's face was neutral.

"Can't the Wild West afford to show some kindness to those less fortunate?" Annie prompted. "It wouldn't cost that much, would it? And it would make such a difference to the children. I know Frank and I, and probably some of the other performers . . ."

A smile came to John Burke's face. Was Burke laughing at her? Hot anger flushed her cheeks. *Were* all white men heartless and crazy?

"A grand gesture—and excellent publicity," Burke said.

Buffalo Bill stroked his goatee and smiled. One eyebrow angled upward. "Good publicity, you say?"

"Without question." Burke rubbed his stubby hands together. "I'll dispatch a wire to the local newspapers. Why, I can picture it now." Burke's stubby hands described imaginary headlines in the air. "WILD WEST DONATES PERFORMANCE TO ORPHANS." Then he muttered, "No, not quite. Needs to be more personal." Burke snapped his fingers, eyes bright with excitement. "We'll call it Annie Oakley Day!"

"That's the ticket!" Buffalo Bill agreed. "We'll start it in New York City. I'll announce it when we do the parade through the streets. If the location's right, we can even make a stop at one of the orphanages. Otherwise we might send a wagon and get some of the children to ride with us in the parade."

The two men were talking so fast, Annie felt a little lost. "So, you're going to do it?"

Buffalo Bill laughed. "Of course! We know better than to argue with a woman who can shoot the flame off a candle."

CHAPTER

7

The parade down Fifth Avenue in New York City was the grandest thing Annie had ever seen. Buffalo Bill pulled out all the stops. People stared in open-mouthed amazement at the wild buffalo, bucking broncos, and dancing Indians as they made their way down to Madison Square Garden.

Annie marveled at the giant indoor stadium. Bear and his crew had decorated the enormous arena with painted backdrops of Western landscapes.

The orphans arrived with long faces, tugging at freshly starched collars. They twisted excitedly under the stern gazes of matrons who marched them into the grandstand in straight, orderly rows.

But as soon as Buffalo Bill galloped into the arena, a spell was cast. Enchanted by the appearance of this real-life legend of the wild West, the children sat breathless and wide-eyed. Some could not control themselves.

"Look out!" a boy shrieked to Shorty, who was about to be jumped by a warrior.

"He's on your left!" a girl chimed in.

The cowboy spun and fired his six-gun. *KABLAM!*
*KABLAM!* The brave dropped to the ground in shud-
dering spasms.

Shorty strode toward the fallen warrior.

"He's only playin' possum!" a boy yelled. "There's
a knife in his boot!"

Shorty chuckled to himself. So much for the staged
knife fight. Standing Deer drew his blade, but Shorty
kicked it out of his hand. He tipped his hat to his
helper in the stands. Now they would have to improvise
a fistfight. Shorty only hoped the powerful Pawnee
would not be too convincing.

"Jab him with your right!" the boy urged.

Annie had no trouble spotting the boy in the stands.
A mop of sandy blond hair hung over his thin face, and
he was grinning in sheer delight.

Then a matron in a high-collared dress and prim
bonnet said sourly, "Hush! That's quite enough. Sit
down."

Annie felt sorry for the boy. Obediently, but with a
"darn it all" shrug, the boy sat back down.

The boy fidgeted in his seat for the rest of the performance. But his eyes danced merrily and seemed to
drink in everything as if it were magic.


After the performance Buffalo Bill clapped Annie on
the back. "That was our best performance yet!"

"Great publicity!" John Burke said as he passed
Annie on his way out of the mess tent.

Even Hugh McCluskey stepped up to congratulate

Annie. But Frank was suspicious of the old man's sudden friendliness. "The old man has a burr in his britches, all right. I heard him grumbling to Bear that there'd never been a Hugh McCluskey Day," Frank whispered. "I think he still resents you."

Annie wanted to believe the old man had finally come around, so she put Frank's words out of her mind.

"Mind if I join you?" McCluskey asked, seating himself at their table.

"Not at all!" Annie said eagerly.

Frank grunted.

"Free tickets for orphans was a great idea," the old man said amiably. "Good publicity."

"That's not why I did it." Annie tried not to sound angry.

"Of course not," McCluskey agreed. "But it never hurts to get your name before the public. That's all part of the sharpshooting game. I should know."

Annie blushed, recalling McCluskey's invitation to help her act her first day in camp. Had she and Frank been rude to ignore the old man? Maybe they'd been wrong about him. "We'd love to hear your suggestions," Annie prompted.

Frank frowned and glared gloomily at the ex-sharpshooter.

McCluskey picked corn from between his teeth and said, "I figure you ought to work in some new tricks, something a bit more challenging. Fer instance, there's no big deal about shooting the heart out've a deck of cards."

Frank pounded his fist on the table. "I'd like to see you try it!"

McCluskey crushed the last bit of his biscuit. "I could and more in my day, sonny," he said smoothly. "Why, I used to shoot a card in half edgewise."

"Edgewise?" Annie was impressed. That *would* be something. She'd never even thought of trying that before.

"Edgewise!" McCluskey said. He rubbed his hands together. "And I used to send a dime spinning in my assistant's fingers, and shoot the tip off a cigarette she held in her mouth."

Frank pushed his plate away and stood up to leave. "Don't believe everything you hear, Annie. Folks have a way of spinning tall tales, especially if they think you're a greenhorn."

"It's all as true as preaching," McCluskey said. "Anyway, I got proof."

McCluskey pulled a leather wallet out of his coat pocket. He carefully unfolded a yellowed poster from a circus that had long since folded its tents. There was a drawing of a slim, handsome man with bushy side-whiskers. The man held a pistol aimed at the smoking cigarette dangling from a pretty girl's mouth.

"Eagle-Eye McCluskey," the poster read, "Champion Sharpshooter of All Time." Suddenly Annie's heart went out to the bent, brittle old man seated across the table. "All Time" hadn't lasted as long as McCluskey had hoped.

"Thank you for your advice, Mr. McCluskey," Annie said gently. "Frank and I will try those tricks you suggested."

The old man nodded, then turned his thin lips up in a grin. "There's no need telling Colonel Cody about this little talk. He loves surprises. Why, the Colonel would be tickled pink if you just slipped some new tricks into yer act."

Frank wasn't so sure. On their way out of the mess tent, Frank warned, "I think McCluskey is trying to trip you up. He'd love to see you miss in front of an audience. And except for the cigarette stunt, I don't think those tricks are humanly possible—not even for you."

Annie's mouth set in a thin but stubborn smile. There was no harm in trying. If she'd been afraid of trying, she never would have learned to shoot in the first place!

So while Frank went to play table tennis with one of the Wichita braves, Annie slipped off with her rifle, an old deck of cards, and several dimes.

Curly was curious why Annie was searching through the logs stacked up behind the mess tent. "Perfect! Exactly what I need." Annie turned to Curly. "May I have this one?"

Curly shrugged his shoulders. "Don't see why not."

The cook scratched his bald head as Annie trotted away, lugging her log. One end had been axed unevenly, leaving a thin blade of wood sticking out. Annie easily split this blade in two.

At the practice range Annie set the log on a bullet-pocked bench in the target area. She then slipped a card in the split blade of wood.

Annie walked a good distance away from the log, loaded her rifle, and fired. *BAM!* Splinters of wood flew off the end of the log.

Annie shook out her shoulders and breathed deeply. She had been too excited; she'd forgotten to take aim!

This time Annie let her rifle rest against her shoulder while she squinted her eyes and focused on the side of the card. The sliver of heavy paper seemed to grow bigger the longer she stared at it. Only then did she fire.

Annie was sure she had missed entirely. Then she realized the card was only half as tall. She had split it straight down the middle—edgewise!

Not bad for a woman, Annie thought. Not bad at all.

Next she set one silver coin in the notched blade of the log, then ran back to the firing line.

*BLAM!*

Annie set the dime spinning on her first try!

Annie practiced for most of the afternoon. Finally, she felt ready to show Frank her new tricks. She smiled and hoisted her rifle to her shoulder. "Keep your eyes on the card, Frank."

"Suit yourself," Frank said. "I still say it can't be done."

Frank whistled when he saw Annie split the card. He could hardly believe what he had just seen, but there it was in his own hand: a card split clean in half . . . edgewise.

"Are you sure you're not worried about losing a few fingers?" Annie asked when Frank picked up the dime.

Frank laughed. "Annie, if you had a mind to, why, I'd let you shoot the lice off my head!" he said.

Annie pretended to consider the thought. "You know, Frank, now that you mention it, the act could use a new—"

Frank threw up his hands. "Now just hold on there, Little Girl."

They both dissolved in laughter.

After a while Frank said, "I sure never would have believed such tricks were possible."

"For a woman?" Annie teased.

Frank smiled. "For *anyone*."

"Maybe we were wrong about McCluskey," Annie said.

"Maybe," Frank said. "Right now, we have some work to do!" Frank was as excited about the new act as Annie was.

"First I've got to get us some cigarettes from Bear," Frank said.

Annie had some ideas of her own about the act. "I was just thinking, Frank," she said. "If I start now, I might be able to finish sewing your new shirt before the next performance. And I think I'll add a row of fringe to the bottom of my skirt."

"That's my Little Girl—new costumes to go with the new act!" Frank said.

Annie hurried off to their tent and her portable sewing machine. When Frank came back with the cigarettes, Annie had him try on the shirt. It was made of a soft blue wool fabric she had purchased a few towns back. The style was modeled on shirts the cowboys wore, double-breasted with a pointed panel over the chest.

Annie pinned on the sleeves and admired her handiwork. "The blue sets off your eyes," she observed happily.

"Don't let that distract you while you're shooting!" Frank teased.

Annie was sewing the brass buttons on Frank's new shirt when the familiar shouts and shinnies and bustle outside told her it was almost time for the afternoon performance.

"Here," Frank said, handing Annie a small mirror.

She looked at the gray-eyed young woman with the thick brown hair. Folks had often called her pretty, especially her smile, but all Annie ever saw was herself. "Do I look all right?" she asked.

Frank smiled and squeezed Annie's hand. "You look a whole heap better than all right, Annie."

"Really?" Annie asked.

"As pretty as a picture," Frank said, staring at her reflection in the mirror.

"Ah, Frank, you're just teasing," Annie said, and playfully pushed away his hand.

Frank feigned innocence. "Why, Miss Annie Oakley," he said. "Did you think I married you only because you were pretty good with a rifle?"

"Pretty good?" Annie protested.

"Very good," Frank amended. Then he added, "Okay, the best."

"That's better," Annie said, and turned her back to Frank and looked at him in the mirror. He was smiling.

"I'm mighty proud of you, Annie Oakley," he said. "Now, come on! Let's go out there and do the impossible!"

The impossible was becoming routine. Annie's act came off without a hitch.

"That was just great, missie!" Buffalo Bill cried after the performance.

"Splendid, indeed!" John Burke said. Annie's ears were still ringing with the roar of gunshots and applause. She was delighted. The new tricks had been a huge success.

"Normally I hate surprises during a performance," Buffalo Bill said. "But you really showed those folks some shooting!"

Annie was confused. McCluskey had told her and Frank that Buffalo Bill *liked* surprises! Suddenly it came to her. She looked at Frank. He had his jaw set in a hard grim line, and Annie knew he was thinking the same thing: the old man had deliberately lied. Annie had no doubts now that McCluskey was also responsible for stealing George.

The voice of John Burke shook her from her thoughts.

"I believe a new poster is in order," John Burke announced dramatically with a sweeping wave of his hands. "We could feature Miss Oakley performing some of her spectacular stunts." Annie was speechless. Everything was happening so fast. It was wonderful and terrifying at the same time.

"Yes, John! That's a splendid idea," Buffalo Bill agreed. "Keep it up, Little Sure Shot, and I may have to give you a raise." Annie grinned so hard it hurt. Frank, too.

But her grin slid from her face the instant she turned and saw Hugh McCluskey stomping away, madder than a wet hen.

CHAPTER
8

When Frank tacked up the new poster on the wall of their tent, Annie stood back with her hands together and frowned. "You don't think it's a little much, do you?" she asked him.

Frank had to smile. He knew Annie loved the new poster as much as he did. Frank stood next to Annie and pretended to give it a critical look. He rubbed his chin thoughtfully. "Well . . ."

Annie turned to him, alarmed. "What? You think it makes me look ugly. Oh, honestly, Frank, sometimes I think I look as homely as a cow."

"Whoa!" Frank said, holding up his hands. "The truth is, Annie, I think it's darn near pretty enough to hang in a museum in Europe."

Annie was pleased. She thought the poster made her look pretty, too. And she loved the nickname that captioned the picture: Little Sure Shot.

Frank flung open the tent flap. "Now Miss Oakley," he said, bowing like a fancy gentleman. "If you're done admiring yourself, would you care to join me for supper? I'm starved."

Outside the mess tent Frank and Annie met Curly. The cook seemed unusually agitated.

"What's wrong, Curly?" Annie asked as they stepped inside.

"Trouble, Annie," he said.

"What kind of trouble?" Frank asked.

"Someone's been stealing things." Annie couldn't believe it. Who in the Wild West would want to steal anything? Especially from a fellow performer.

"Things are missing from around the compound," Curly explained. "I've lost a pie a day since we left New York City. Colorado Jack's missing a blanket. And some no-account low-down thievin' varmint even swiped Shorty's lucky shirt right off the clothesline!" Annie could not help but notice that Curly's language was even spicier than his chili.

She asked Shorty when he'd last seen his shirt.

"On the clothesline yesterday after lunch," Shorty said. "I knew it was dry, but there was a poker game going on, so I figured I'd take it down later."

Colorado Jack patted his friend's shoulder. "Soon as we get paid, I'll buy you a new one."

"Much obliged, Jack," Shorty said. "But it won't be the same!" He sounded like a little boy who'd lost his favorite toy.

Annie understood. Performers were superstitious about things like clothing. She'd known a clown in the

Sells Brothers Circus who wore the same pair of socks for every performance, even after they practically became rags. Without those socks he was a ball of nerves. But once that clown pulled on his lucky socks, he was ready for anything. Annie figured that must be how Shorty felt about his missing shirt.

"What did your shirt look like?" she asked.

"It was blue, ma'am," Shorty said, "with brass buttons."

Hugh McCluskey rudely pushed his way forward.

"Just like the one her husband wore yesterday," he said with a nasty sneer.

Suddenly Annie found herself being stared at from all sides. "That's ridiculous!" Frank said.

"That's right," Annie said. "How could Frank wear Shorty's shirt? The sleeves would be up to his elbows." As preposterous as the accusation seemed, Annie was stunned by the embarrassing silence of her fellow performers. How could they believe she would steal? Annie wondered. But rumors are like brush fires in July. All it takes is the tiniest spark, and, once it's started, it's the devil's time stopping it.

"I made Frank that shirt," Annie insisted. "I can show you the scraps of leftover fabric." McCluskey jumped in like a man fanning a flame.

"Trouble didn't start till after she joined the company," McCluskey said. His eyes glided meaningfully from one face to the next. A few men grumbled or tugged at their chins as if to say the old man was right.

Finally, Bear decided he'd heard enough.

"Why would Annie steal pies?" he demanded. "That don't make sense."

"Doesn't have to," McCluskey answered smoothly. "Some rich people steal just for the heck of it. My cousin owns a grocery, said his worst pincher was the richest woman in town. Got so he had to follow her around the store."

A mutter of assent spread through the gathered crew members.

McCluskey could feel the flames of suspicion building and sweeping through the crowd. "We really don't know anything about Miss Oakley, do we?" he said. "Maybe she didn't *quit* the Sells Brothers Circus. Maybe she was *fired* for stealing!"

"Now hold on there!" Frank was white hot with anger. "You can't go accusing someone without any proof."

"Who said I don't have proof?" McCluskey suggested. His gray eyes gleamed triumphantly. "The proof's right here by the cooling rack."

Frank looked stunned.

McCluskey pointed to a boot print dried into the mud beneath the rack. Frank pressed forward to examine the print.

"That's too small to belong to any man," McCluskey said. His mouth curled into a malicious grin, and Annie flinched at the sight of his tobacco-stained teeth. "But it's just about right for *her* dainty foot, isn't it?"

Annie was so angry that tears sprang to her eyes.

How could anyone tell such lies? And, even worse, how could anyone *believe* them?

Frank, fists clenched, stepped toward McCluskey. "I've heard all the lies I'm gonna hear from you, old man," Frank said. "It's time we settle this, once and for all."

"That's enough now!" Everyone seemed to freeze, including Frank.

Annie realized, gratefully, that the voice coming from the back of the tent belonged to Buffalo Bill.

"We've all got to work together," Cody said calmly. The crowd parted as he passed, with John Burke right behind. "So just keep a watch on your things and a button on your lips. I won't have rumors tearing apart my Wild West."

The crowd reluctantly broke into small, muttering groups and returned to work.

Cody put a strong hand on Annie's shoulder. "Don't worry, missie," he said gently. "This storm will blow over. They all do."

John Burke explained, "I'm afraid your success has excited jealous feelings among your fellow performers."

Frank reassuringly squeezed Annie's hand. Annie managed a little smile.

"That's better," Cody said. "Now, why don't you two forget all about this and go enjoy your lunch."

Annie realized Cody was right. There was no sense letting foolish gossip upset her. After all, Annie had been through a lot worse in her life. She decided to keep her head high and her eyes open.

# CHAPTER 9

It was over a plate of roast grouse that Annie suddenly had an idea.

"Why didn't I think of it sooner?" she exclaimed, her eyes glowing with excitement.

Frank wiped the grease from his fingers. "Think of what?"

"We'll set a trap for the thief," Annie explained. The grouse had reminded her of her days long ago, even before she had learned to shoot. Bored with a diet of bread and nuts, Annie had built traps to catch grouse, quail, and rabbits near the cabin.

"But what kind of trap would you set for a thief?" Annie mumbled to herself. She couldn't exactly lay a trail of corn kernels up to a cage made of sticks and reeds.

"Aren't you going to eat your dessert?" Frank asked.

"That's it!" Annie cried.

Frank nearly jumped clear out of his chair.

"Dessert! That's our bait. The thief likes pies," Annie explained.

Frank faked a look of disappointment.

"Does that mean I don't get your slice of pie?"

Annie and Frank waited for hours in front of the mess tent. Curly had seen the sense in Annie's plan and had set out several fresh pies to cool on a bench outside the tent.

The sweet smell of apples and cinnamon floated on the cool night wind. A bright half-moon had risen, but its light came and went with the clouds blown on the breeze.

"If the thief doesn't steal those pies soon, I will!" Frank whispered.

Annie didn't answer. Frank looked down and saw she was sleeping beside him, crouched behind one of Curly's giant kettles. Annie clutched her rifle in her arms like a doll.

Frank sighed. "I'm too hungry to fall asleep."

Just then he heard the muffled sound of someone creeping on tiptoe. Frank froze, every muscle tense, listening. Yes, they were definitely footsteps!

Straining to make out the shape in the darkness, Frank nudged Annie awake and signaled for her to be quiet. Her mouth opened in sleepy surprise, but no sound escaped. Her hands were ready on the trigger almost before her eyes were fully open.

Finally, the clouds drifted free of the moon. Annie took aim at her target. The figure that appeared in the light was not whom she expected.

"He's just a boy!" she exclaimed, and lowered her gun.

Suddenly the boy dropped the pie and ran. "Hold it right there!" Frank shouted, and he ran after him. "Follow him, Annie!" Annie sprang into a gallop, but the boy was as quick and shifty as a scared rabbit.

"Whoa there, boy!" Frank hollered.

"We won't hurt you," Annie called out.

As fast as Frank and Annie were, they were no match for a panicked boy. Frank dragged himself to a stop. He was breathing hard.

"We'll never catch him like this," Annie said. Frank agreed.

"Tell you what," Frank managed to say between puffs. "You head out that way, and I'll go this way." Annie understood. Frank meant to trap the boy between them.

The fact was, Annie had considerable experience tracking down the likes of squirrels, rabbits, and such. Scrappy boys, however, were an altogether different animal. This boy was as fast as lightning and as slippery as a greased pig. And he had already proved he knew his way in and around the camp.

Suddenly Annie heard footsteps. She pressed herself against a tent wall. She would count to three, she decided, and then throw a bear tackle around the boy. She counted. "One . . . two . . . three!" In a flash she jumped. He fell over backward with a startled "Oooomph!" as Annie pinned him to the ground.

Then there was a terrific roar of laughter. Annie blinked. "Frank?"

Frank was laughing so hard the noise brought several people out of their tents to see what all the commotion was about. Frank twisted out from under Annie and dusted himself off. "Tarnation, Annie," he said. A huge grin spread across his face. "I knew you could shoot better than any man. But I didn't know you could wrestle bear, too!"

They both dissolved into fits of laughter. They had almost forgotten about the thief until Sitting Bull spoke from the entrance of his tent.

"The boy is inside," he said. "His name is Hawkeye."

# CHAPTER 10

A nnie and Frank slipped inside Sitting Bull's tent. By the candle's flickering flame, Annie examined the boy's face. He looked familiar. Annie suddenly remembered. This was the boy who had "helped" Shorty during the battle for the Deadwood Stage.

The boy wiped his nose on the sleeve of Shorty's lucky blue shirt.

"It does get awfully cold at night around here," Annie said gently. But the boy's eyes shifted nervously away from her gaze.

"What's all the ruckus?" came a voice from outside.

Annie smiled. Nothing happened in the Wild West without Buffalo Bill finding out about it.

He stepped into the circle of light. Cody's long hair was sleep tossed, but his gun belt was strapped at the ready over his wrinkled nightshirt.

"We caught the thief," Frank explained.

Buffalo Bill stroked his pointed beard. "I don't see any thief. All I see is a boy. What's your name, son?"

"Hawkeye."

"That's not much of a name. Don't you have an-other?" Buffalo Bill asked.

The boy folded his arms over his chest and shook his head.

"Did you run away from home, son?"

Hawkeye shook his head.

"Can't you talk?"

Hawkeye looked down at his feet and mumbled, "Don't have no home."

"An orphan, huh?"

Hawkeye's chin poked up defiantly. "Ain't no or-phan, neither. Don't need a home. I'm old enough to work."

Annie looked the boy up and down. She guessed he was about ten years old, the age she had been when she'd left the poorhouse to work for that mean farmer. It was a dangerous age. Greedy people knew they could get away with cheating a child who was on his or her own.

"Don't you think your folks are worried about you?" Annie asked gently.

"Don't have any folks," the boy said, turning away from all their staring eyes.

"I thought you said you weren't an orphan," Frank said.

"My pa ain't dead," Hawkeye said. "He just dumped me in the orphanage after Ma died."

Annie figured Hawkeye said he had no last name be-cause he didn't want anything to do with the father who had deserted him. She couldn't really blame him.

"I ain't stayin' there, and nobody can make me!" Hawkeye concluded.

"I will take the boy home to my tribe," Sitting Bull said.

Annie recalled Shorty telling her that in a blizzard, cattle turn tail, while buffalo plow ahead and face the gale. That was Sitting Bull—as stubborn as a buffalo. No one could force him to turn his back on a child.

"Is that what you want?" Buffalo Bill asked Hawkeye.

"I want to be a sharpshooter in your Wild West show," the boy said.

Buffalo Bill put a hand on the boy's shoulder and leaned down to look Hawkeye right in the eyes. "Can't blame you for wanting to be in the Wild West, son. And I'll be glad to hire you when you're old enough."

Annie glanced at Frank. He'd been only a few years older than Hawkeye when he'd come to America all alone to escape the hard times following the Irish potato famine. Frank had worked many odd jobs, from stableboy to newsboy, before finally teaching himself to be a sharpshooter so he could earn better pay.

"That's not a bad plan," Annie said.

"If you're willing to practice long hours and work hard," Frank agreed.

"All's I need is a gun and bullets . . . and someone to teach me." Hawkeye risked a glance in Annie's direction.

"You also need a home," Annie corrected. "A place to go to school and someone to take care of you."

"Then I'll live with the chief," Hawkeye said.

Sitting Bull looked at Buffalo Bill. The old scout yawned. "All right. The boy can stay in your tent until the end of the season. And I'll tell Curly to keep him in pies."

Annie threw her arms around Buffalo Bill's neck and kissed his cheek.

Cody smiled. "Well, well! A peck like that can only mean sweet dreams, so good night! I'll see you all in the morning."

"Good night, Colonel Cody!" Hawkeye said. His face looked about to split in half from grinning.

After Frank had turned down the lantern, Annie whispered into the darkness, "Do you think Hawkeye will do all right living with the Sioux?"

Frank yawned. "He'll probably like it better than the orphanage, and I can't think of another solution."

As she listened to Frank's gentle snoring, Annie turned the problem over and over in her mind. I wonder if Frank's right, Annie thought. Then the answer came to her as a bolt of lightning.

The next morning the whole compound was buzzing with the news of the stowaway boy.

Curly heaped Hawkeye's tray with eggs and biscuits and said, "A growing boy can't live on just pies."

"But they're such good pies," Hawkeye said.

Curly beamed. "I add plenty of cinnamon. And I don't skimp on the lard, neither," he said, wagging a ladle in the boy's face.

Hawkeye had just made another friend.

As soon as breakfast was over, Annie brought Hawkeye to the tent shared by Shorty and Colorado Jack. Hawkeye returned Jack's blanket. But before he could touch a brass button on the shirt, Shorty stopped him.

"You don't have to return it," the cowboy said. "The shirt fits you good, and maybe it'll bring you as much luck to wear it as it will for me to give it."

Annie gave Shorty a quick hug. The cowboy blushed to his roots.

"He can keep my blanket, too!" Colorado Jack said. "I need all the luck I can git. Maybe now I'll beat Shorty at poker."

Annie laughed and hugged him, too.

Then Hawkeye asked if Shorty and Jack would be willing to show him a few rope tricks. The cowboys were delighted to have a chance to show off their skills.

By lunchtime Hawkeye had made a whole passel of friends. He wore a string of Wichita friendship beads around his neck, and an eagle feather poked from the flat black vaquero's hat on his head. When Hawkeye strolled by, everyone stopped to say "Howdy"—everyone except the one person Annie had hoped would take an interest in the boy.

"Looks like I'm going to have to take matters into my own hands," Annie muttered to herself.

"No sense wasting good conversation on your lonesome, Miss Annie," Bear teased.

Annie had been so preoccupied she hadn't noticed the big roustabout walking alongside her.

"I'd be glad to chew the fat with you till it's time to get ready for the afternoon performance," Bear said.

"I don't know if you can help," she said. "How do you get someone who's as stubborn and contrary as a mule to do something for their own good?"

Bear scratched his thick brown beard. "Make like you don't want him to do it," he said finally. "Why, once I had a dog that would never sit unless I told him to roll over. And the only way my ma ever got me to eat my peas was by telling me she'd rather I wouldn't so she could give them to my brother."

"That's it!" Annie cried. "Bear, can you do me a favor after the performance?"

"Just name it," Bear said. "As long as it doesn't mean eating peas."

Annie kept glancing over her shoulder between firing shots at the practice range.

"What's the matter, Mrs. Oakley? Is yer neck botherin' ya?" Hawkeye asked.

"No, I'm fine," Annie said. But her brows were knit with worry. Where was Bear?

"Aren't you going to let me try?" Hawkeye asked.

Annie knew the boy's fingers were itching to pull the trigger, but if all went according to plan, the boy would be up to his ankles in bullet casings in no time. If only Bear would show up already.

Annie's face relaxed into a smile. Bear was lumbering toward them, with McCluskey in tow.

"Don't see what you need me fer," the old man

grumbled. "But I'm glad to be useful to someone, I suppose."

"It's the, uh, targets, Mr. McCluskey. I, um, wanted your advice before I painted up some fresh ones," Bear lied. His round cheeks blushed red.

Now or never, Annie thought. She turned to Hawkeye. "I'm sorry, but I haven't got time to teach you to shoot, and neither does Frank. It's a real shame that Mr. McCluskey is too old to give you lessons."

McCluskey strode over to Annie. "Who's too old!" he demanded.

"Oh, I meant no disrespect," Annie said hastily. She crossed her fingers behind her back.

"Jest because I'm too old for the ring—in some people's opinion—don't mean I can't show this young'un a trick or two!" McCluskey roared. "Can we borrow yer rifle for a moment, Miss Oakley?"

Annie eagerly handed her gun to McCluskey. While the old man was busy showing Hawkeye the right way to brace it against his shoulder, Annie winked at Bear and whispered, "Thanks!"

By the time Hawkeye returned Annie's rifle, old McCluskey was calling him "son" and praising the boy's "natural-born marksmanship."

"He'll be better than you in no time, Miss Oakley," McCluskey boasted. "No offense—but shooting is a manly art."

Annie knew better than to argue.

# CHAPTER 11

**T**own after town glided past the windows of the Wild West train. Green leaves turned to red and gold and gathered in crackling piles along the tracks and around the tent poles. Annie was surprised to realize it was already October—the end of the performing season.

Annie and Frank had worked up something special for the final performance. Near the end of their act, Frank made an announcement. "Ladies and gentlemen, it is our privilege to introduce to you a promising young sharpshooter making his Wild West debut—Hawkeye!"

The boy ran into the ring accompanied by a warm round of applause.

Hawkeye whispered to Frank, who held up his hands for quiet.

"Ladies and gentlemen," Frank shouted, "I give you Hawkeye . . . McCluskey!"

Annie grinned. So the old coot had made the adoption official. She was glad. According to Sitting Bull, a new name meant a new life. She hoped this one would be happier for Hawkeye.

The applause died down as Hawkeye readied himself. Finally, he nodded. Frank tossed several clay targets up in the air.

*BAM! BAM! BA-DAM!*

A rain of clay dust splattered the ground. The crowd roared its approval. Then Frank held an ace of hearts in his hand.

Annie crossed her fingers and silently prayed. "Please don't miss!" She hoped no one saw her shut her eyes.

Hawkeye took careful aim, squeezed the trigger, and . . . *BAM!*

Annie opened her eyes at the sound of loud claps and whistles. Hawkeye had shot the heart right out of the ace!

Now it was Annie's turn. Frank turned the card edgewise, and Annie lifted her rifle to shoot.

A hush fell over the spectators. Frank was amazed that so many people could be so quiet, but Annie didn't notice; her world had shrunk to the sliver of paper in Frank's hand.

*BAM!*

The ace was sliced in half—edgewise!

Annie took Hawkeye's hand and ran happily to Frank. She waved for the old man watching in the wings to join them.

Hugh McCluskey hesitated, then shuffled into the arena. Annie clasped his hand with her free one. Hands linked, the sharpshooters—young, old, and in between—raised their arms together in triumph. Then, to thunderous applause, they took a bow.

# EPILOG

*Annie Oakley was one of the best sharpshooters of all time—perhaps the best. At the peak of her show business career with Buffalo Bill's Wild West, Annie was one of the most popular entertainers in the world. In one winter tour alone more than one million spectators crowded Madison Square Garden to see Little Sure Shot, and it is estimated that seventy million people saw the show worldwide. In Paris jubilant crowds cheered, "Viva Annie!" When the Wild West traveled to London for Queen Victoria's jubilee celebration, the queen congratulated Annie personally.*

*As recounted in this book, Annie actually could shoot the ash off a cigarette, the heart out of a playing card, or an apple off her pet poodle George's head while on horseback! For audiences throughout the world, the Little Girl of the Western Plains was a real-life folk heroine. Her beginnings, however, were anything but grand.*

*Phoebe Anne Moses was born August 13, 1860, in Darke County, Ohio. Her family was desperately poor. In an attempt to fend off starvation, Annie was sent to work—at age nine—at a poorhouse forty miles from home. Later she learned how to trap* game, and she sold the meat in town to help pay off the mortgage on the family farm. Two years later Annie picked up her stepfather's rifle and discovered she could shoot. It was not until Annie was fifteen years old, however, and staying with her sister in Cincinnati, that her sharpshooting skills gained her any celebrity. A famous marksman named Frank Butler offered $100 to anyone who could beat him in a contest. Annie accepted the challenge. It was the easiest $100 Annie ever made.

A little more than a year later Annie and Frank were married. The Butlers formed a sharpshooting act and for a number of years toured the East on the vaudeville circuit and in circuses. In 1885 they joined Buffalo Bill's Wild West. For seventeen years Annie was one of its biggest stars. She met and befriended many famous people, including the Sioux chief Sitting Bull. Unlike popular legend on which this novel is based, however, recent evidence suggests that Sitting Bull joined the show after Annie had. But Sitting Bull did adopt her as his "daughter."

Economic hard times and the popularity of new—and cheaper—forms of entertainment would mean the end of western shows. In 1902, Annie and Frank retired from the Wild West and settled in North Carolina and Florida. In 1926 she and Frank moved back home to Ohio. Annie died that year at the age of sixty-six. Frank died twenty days later.

Through countless books, plays, comics, television shows, and movies, the legend of Annie Oakley lives on.